# Reboot

## LK WOLLETT

Published by LK WOLLETT, 2023.

# Reboot - Laura
# By LK Wollett
# Chapter 1
# Parental Discretion Advised

"Smith Jamison," I grumbled as I walked out of the meeting room. "What kind of name is that anyway? A clerical error?"

"Aaaaghhhh", my supervisor, Amy, growled. "He is the most obnoxious man!"

Both of us were steaming at his roadblock of our plan to streamline the accounting system.

"We weren't asking for more money," Amy preached to me, the choir.

"Or more help!" I joined in. "It wasn't his idea, so..."

"Right," Amy agreed as we turned to enter our offices.

Rather than sitting down, I walked to the ladies' room and he was coming down the hall; a little taller than me, his muscular arms bulging under his tight shirt. The popular five o'clock shadow covered his square jaw, and light brown hair covered his head except for a bald spot on top toward the back. His squinty reptile eyes were always turned away and his thin-lipped mouth didn't smile much. In conversations that I wasn't a part of, he mentioned a son and I heard he went to Europe with a girl friend. Why I was attracted to him, I could not figure out, but I was drawn to him like a paperclip to a magnet.

He saw me in the hall and I stiffened.

"Laura," he acknowledged as he passed by, peering at me with those squinty eyes.

Back at my desk, I opened emails. Past meetings with Smith were running through my mind. Today's meeting was a request to post data on an internal website and I knew what I wanted. He, however, even though unfamiliar with the Accounting Department, had his own ridiculous version. After debating with him for an hour, I ran out of patience and lost my temper, shouting at him that I didn't want him to be involved. I abruptly walked out and Amy followed.

At closing time, I got interested in a project and stayed a little longer than usual. When I realized the time, I walked to my car in the company's empty parking lot. Smith was walking briskly from the VP parking section, heading directly toward me. With dread, I waited for him leaning on the driver's side of my car, wondering if he wanted to berate me.

"Laura," he began, a little breathless, as he stopped in front of me.

I looked up at him waiting for his verbal assault. With no warning, he grabbed a tuft of my hair at the back of my head, bent down and gently stroked his lips on mine. More alarming than his kiss was my reaction. Every cell in my body wanted to strip so he could have his way. Letting go of my hair, his hands slid down my back and his thumbs touched my breasts. Putting my hands on his shoulders, I finally pushed him away.

"What are you doing?" I bellowed, looking down, hiding my reaction.

"The lady doth protest?" he asked and actually broke a tilted smile.

"Of course, I protest!" I cried turning to open the door.

Putting his hand on top of the car, he leaned close to me.

"You're attracted to me," he declared. "I see you talking to men all day like they were trees but when you talk to me, you ignite."

Though it would remain my secret forever, he was right. My phone rang.

"Oh, hi, Donald," I said then I opened the car door looking at Smith defiantly. "This is my fiancé. Have a good night."

A few blocks from the parking lot, I pulled to the curb to talk to Donald. My body was trembling slightly from the adrenaline rush, I guess, or whatever happens when sexually aroused.

"Yes, I'm heading home now," I answered, a quiver in my voice.

"What's wrong?" Donald demanded.

"Smith Jamison," I began with a sigh then paused, a little worried about Donald's reaction.

"What is it?" Donald urged, sounding worried.

"He kissed me," I recounted flatly though a bolt of lightening shot through me.

"Kissed you?" Donald responded with indignation.

Having known Donald for five years, I could guess his expression. His intense blue eyes would be envisioning the scene. His sculpted, clean-shaven face would be tense, jaws clenched. His lean, 6 foot frame, poised for action.

"Yes," I sighed. "I don't know what got into him. We had a meeting today and he was his same obnoxious self."

"I don't want you to go back there," Donald blurted.

"I can't just quit," I wailed.

"You can," Donald insisted. "Report him to Personnel and give your notice."

Without promising I would do as he asked, I told him I was tired and would see him later. When I got to my apartment, Donald was waiting for me with a bag of food from my favorite restaurant. Then I walked toward my door and he pulled me close. While every cell in my body wasn't screaming to strip, a warm glow overcame me. It was a glow that felt safe and steady. I loved it. At the kitchen table, he talked again about my quitting.

"You're not safe there," he argued. "Those sexual urges can get out of control."

Unfortunately, I blushed and he noticed.

"You know I'm right," Donald pressed. "We have both seen our friends burn with lust and die."

He was right though he didn't mean 'die' physically; he meant the relationship died. The friends he referred to was at a church near our secular college campus. We met at a 'tea' hosted by the church to welcome new students. Donald stood apart from every other student because he was clean and pressed. No jeans, certainly no torn jeans, no tee shirts; always slacks and an upscale golf shirt.

"I know, I know," I agreed nodding. "But I'm aware of Smith's 'urges' now and I'll stay away from him."

Donald wasn't having it. He leaned toward me and put his hand on my arm.

"You were going to quit anyway, weren't you?" Donald asked looking panicked. "We wanted our first baby right away?"

What he said was true. This was our plan.

"I guess I didn't realize I would go through transition pains," I admitted. "The moment of truth is here, isn't it?"

He was looking at me with compassion and worry. There was no doubt that I was important to him; that I was his treasure. In a month, I would be his wife. Why he chose me out of the hundreds of girls he met at college, only God knows.

At work the next day, I told Amy I was leaving. While she expressed surprise that this was sooner than expected, we knew this day was coming and we were prepared. Plastic bag in hand, I took a few personal items off my desk and said 'good-bye' to my career. Mr. Smith Jamison was nowhere to be seen.

# Chapter 2

How God works sometimes is unfathomable. After five years, all my pregnancies miscarried. Donald and I were heartbroken but we accepted that this was God's will. We turned to adoption and found three related orphans: Joanie, age 6; Andrew, age 4, and Sam, age 3.

Donald's good income as a sales manager made it possible to send Joanie to a Christian school. Unfortunately, when they tested her, she was so far behind, they started her in kindergarten rather than first grade. Spending a lot of time with her at home trying to help her catch up, she showed no interest in lessons and both of us were getting burned out. Hoping to find something as an incentive, I signed her up for soccer.

At the first practice, having purchased and outfitted all of the children in soccer uniforms and gear, we got out of the van and found her team. The boys wouldn't be playing but they soon found other children their age to play with. Joanie's team had gathered on the sidelines with their coaches; some older boys were on the field. Parents on the other side of the field were being quite vocal.

"F-you," a man cursed. "F-you, Davis."

Glancing up, my eyes focused on the man.

"Was that Smith Jamison?" I thought to myself, wishing I had binoculars.

Watching him pace as he watched one of the boys, he walked like Smith. He turned around to talk to someone and there was his bald spot. The cells in my body had no problem remembering his kiss five years ago. Wanting to turn off the memory, I walked back to Joanie and her team.

That night, Donald worked late, as he did often. I was exhausted, as usual, after homework and getting the children bathed and in bed so I fell asleep as soon as I laid down. I wasn't aware when Donald lay beside me or kissed me on the cheek. The next morning, he was already gone and he would be gone for a few days. He left a note: "We need to get away. Tell me when."

This made me smile and I knew exactly where I wanted to go: the same beach as our honeymoon. Thirty days later, as we checked into the hotel, I was saddened that all I felt was tired, so unlike that wondrous wedding night, five years ago, when excitement pulsed through our bodies, knowing a completely new experience was about to occur. Through that week of our honeymoon, our energy seem boundless as we swam, snorkeled, sailed and savored every sexual moment. Tonight, I was hungry for food and sleep.

After we had supper in the hotel restaurant, we went to our room where Donald took my hand, led me to the balcony and beckoned me to sit with him.

"I think I failed you," Donald stated.

I gasped with shock and started to protest.

"Hush, now," he responded. "Let me finish."

He brought my hand to his heart and closed his eyes.

"When we were engaged, I prayed for you daily at least," he began. "I prayed for God's will to be done in you, in us."

He sighed and leaned back in his chair, looking at the sunset.

"With demands of this job, the house, the children...all of it," Donald continued, "my prayers became occasional and they usually were requesting help with work."

This was embarrassing because I didn't have a prayer life. While we attended church on Sundays, I realized, with Donald's confession, that God was not a part of my daily life.

"You're tired; you're burnt out," Donald observed. "Three children at once was too much."

I nodded. Putting his arm around my shoulders, he kissed the side of my head. Then he prayed.

"Dear Father," he began, "I pray for your will to be done in Laura and me. I'm sorry for neglecting her, Lord. I'm sorry I let worldly responsibilities take precedence. Help me be the husband she deserves."

"Same for me, Lord," I added. "Same for me."

Feeling the glow of God's love, our lips came together, igniting a passion both of us longed for. At the end of our vacation, we vowed to put God first in our life and let him handle our marriage, our work and our family. And we were going to hire a housekeeper/nanny.

# Chapter 3

Let it be known there are few nannies like those portrayed in story books. Nannies we hired left after a few months or they had family problems or health problems, or we just didn't get along. In addition, we were devastated to be told by our tax accountant that we had responsibility for benefits like health and retirement. The end result was an expense much greater than we expected. Donald's income couldn't handle it.

His response was to put Joanie in public school and work harder, leaving me with the children and the current nanny issues. My response was to cut back on everything possible: low cost home-cooked meals, no restaurants, thrift stores for all of us, hand-me-downs for the children, no costly entertainment. Donald even gave up his sports station. The one thing I kept was soccer because it was the one thing that interested Joanie. In her second season, the coach turned to Joanie to assist with the inexperienced players; Joanie seemed to bask in the responsibility.

One afternoon at the soccer field, I heard "F-you" in the crowd; it was Smith. Feeling certain he wouldn't notice me, it was fun watching him from afar, remembering his kiss and letting the cells in my body react. All harmless, yes?

The next day, getting up to start the morning routine, I was shocked to see Donald at the kitchen table, waiting for me.

"What's wrong?" I asked. "Are you alright?"

Donald looked at me intently.

"I was going to ask you the same thing," he answered solemnly.

"I'm as good as you can expect," I responded, sitting across from him. "Things aren't easy now, you know."

Donald nodded; his worried expression more worried than usual.

"You were talking in your sleep," Donald finally stated. "You were groaning, actually."

He shifted a little, cleared his throat and leaned toward me.

"You were talking to Smith," he revealed. "You did this before, last year."

He wanted honesty from me and I didn't want him to have it. Yet I knew he would insist on it, if not verbally, then subtly. My face reddened.

"He was at soccer," I began and I raised my voice a little, "on the other side of the field. He was cursing at one of the players - maybe his son."

"That's it?" Donald demanded. "You just 'saw' him?"

I shifted a little, cleared my throat and leaned back.

"He's nothing to me," I declared searching for an explanation of my body's reaction. "He's a dessert that I can't have."

Donald chuckled, breaking the tension.

"That's a good one," he smiled. "Can I use that sometime?"

"Absolutely not!" I cried with a laugh of relief.

Walking to him, I put my hand on his shoulder and leaned down to look in his eyes.

"You are my main meal," I assured. "My sustenance."

"Am I meat loaf and mashed potatoes?" he asked, looking up at me impishly.

I sat on his lap.

"No, My Darling," I cooed placing my hand on his face. "You are filet mignon with grilled asparagus."

When I caressed his lips, he inhaled deeply, responding in kind, and, wrapping me in his strength, drew me as close as he could. A door opened; the children were getting up.

"Would you go to dinner with me?" he begged as though I might reject him.

"Your wish is my command, Sir," I responded.

Little Andrew scampered into the room with Sam close behind. I picked up one and Donald the other. Asking them about breakfast, Joanie joined us and put her arm on Donald's shoulder, leaning against him. He didn't get to see them like he used to and they spent some time catching up. These moments filled me with that warm glow that I loved.

# Chapter 4

In John chapter 3, where the famous John 3:16 resides, Jesus described the Holy Spirit as a wind[1] that you can hear but you can't tell where it comes from or where it is going. That's how I would describe Abigail, the latest nanny. A young looking woman though nearing forty, she appeared at church one Sunday, a relative of a couple, Norma and John, that Donald and I socialized with occasionally. Abigail was visiting or actually 'retreating' after the death of her husband in a tragic accident. Their one son, with his wife, missionaries, were stationed in India where communications were limited. Meeting her for the first time, she had a glowing countenance but the pain of her loss was apparent. Thinking of losing Donald in the same way, it was easy to empathize. On this Sunday, the couple asked us to go to a buffet with them. Normally, Donald and I would decline for financial reasons but for God's reasons, I guess, Donald was agreeable therefore I was, too.

In the buffet line, as I was attempting to cater to the children's wants, Abigail walked next to Joanie and said something that made Joanie giggle. Seeing Joanie smile made me smile. As Joanie sat at the table next to Donald, Abigail took on Andrew who wanted all sweets. Somehow, without argument, Abigail got corn on his plate and some chicken fingers. She escorted Andrew back to the table. By that time, Sam's plate was filled and he was seated. Abigail and I stood together at the buffet.

"You are great with children!" I declared.

"You think so?" she responded modestly.

"Absolutely!" I affirmed. "I never would have gotten a vegetable on Andrew's plate."

Looking over at Andrew, he was actually eating the corn.

"A gift from God, I guess," Abigail explained. "We can praise him for that."

Something about her glowed; it was fascinating.

"Norma said you need a nanny," Abigail offered.

My body reacted with joy like she had offered me a zillion dollars!

"You're interested?" I blurted with amazement.

Abigail nodded and walked to the table; I followed.

"I need something to do," Abigail explained. "That big house..."

She looked away as sadness filled her face.

"You don't want to work?" I inquired knowing I would want to work.

"Roger's estate paid for the house and car," Abigail continued. "I don't need the money...or the hassle. I worked before we were married and..."

"I know what you mean," I interrupted. "You have to love the job."

"If I sell the house, I probably won't need money," she stated.

"Where do you live?" I wondered in amazement.

She told me the location but I wasn't familiar with it. I assumed it was high-scale if the proceeds would make her rich. Andrew joined us and he lifted his arms to Abigail; she drew him onto her lap. He leaned on her, relaxed, peaceful. In our van, on the way home, I told Donald about Abigail. Later that day, her luxury car that looked like the latest model, pulled into the driveway. Donald asked questions and she was soon relaying to him what she had told me. Andrew appeared in the living room door and scampered to her. She cooed something to him and he smiled. Sam, who was never far away from Andrew, joined us, sitting on my lap, and then Joanie came in who leaned against Donald. With all of them as witnesses, I invited Abigail to be our nanny and she accepted.

Donald was working and Joanie was at school when Abigail drove again into our driveway with suitcases and an old trunk almost as tall as me. It fascinated the boys; they tinkered with the locks trying to get it open. Abigail let us stay with her as she unpacked. She had a way of making conversation that was light-hearted and easy to listen to. Finally, the trunk came open to reveal her Sunday dresses and suits hanging on the left side; drawers were on the right. The boys opened the drawers to discover their contents but Abigail didn't make them stop; she instead explained what they were looking at. The biggest drawer at the bottom contained children's books. Sparking excitement, the boys each took one, sat on the floor and looked at pictures.

When Abigail's room was arranged, the children and I gave her a tour of the house. In the kitchen, we stopped to make lunch. When the boys were done they went into the back yard; Abigail and I cleaned up and joined them. The next couple of hours flew by as we played some hide-and-seek, some tag and a toddler version of soccer. Joanie joined us meaning it was time to go to the real soccer fields.

Once again the older boys were on the field and Smith was cursing.

"Who is that?" Abigail asked looking at Smith.

"Smith Jamison," I answered flatly. "I used to work with him."

"He's a devil, that one," Abigail declared as she walked away.

"You got that right," I agreed, following her, and I shared what he did to me.

"He pulled your hair?" Abigail cried. "And you're lusting after him?"
I gasped.

"Am I lusting?" I exclaimed with a slight laugh but she was dead serious.

"You're committing adultery!" she accused.

"He's a hundred yards away!" I retorted, still wanting to laugh at her.

"Do you read your Bible, Missy?" she challenged. "Matthew 5:28, Jesus said if you look at someone with lust, you have committed adultery."[2]

Anger rose in me; the first angry response I had felt toward Abigail.

"Don't be gettin' mad at me," she demanded. "Jesus said it. Take it to him."

As we drove home, I was thinking about lust. When everyone got out of the van, I lingered, closed my eyes and asked God to forgive me and help me.

In the house, we started meal preparations. When Abigail invited Joanie to help, she complied to my surprise. As Abigail patiently instructed Joanie, I realized how much patience I was lacking. Though I was mature enough to appreciate what Abigail was doing for Joanie, I immaturely felt inadequate and useless. I wanted Donald who seemed to treasure me no matter what.

With the children fed, it was time for the homework battle that occurred nightly. Hoping for a miracle, I invited Abigail to give it a try. Walking into the family room, I announced it was bath time which, thankfully, the boys enjoyed. Sitting next to the tub, we played a little with their bath toys and I got them scrubbed. In their bedroom, Andrew brought me one of Abigail's books and we cuddled on the floor to read it.

Hearing the shower, I assumed the homework battle was done and Joanie was getting ready for bed. Coaxing the boys into bed, promising them a story in the morning, I turned out the light and went to find Abigail. She was sitting on the deck and I decided not to disturb her.

Checking on Joanie who was in bed, I leaned down to say good night. She reached up to hug me and I knelt to let her know how much I loved her. This loving exchange and the peace of this entire night was a direct result of Abigail fighting the homework battle. Normally by this time, Joanie and I were cranky and I was too tired to coax anyone let alone two small boys.

In my room, I showered and, rather than falling asleep immediately, I opened a book. Donald came in and expressed delight that I was up as he entered the bathroom. He then slipped into bed and took the book out of my hand. He uttered surprise at my negligee and made a reference to 'ice cream', because he described my breasts as 'ice cream cones'. I touched him the way I knew he liked. After a while he moaned and quivered as his kisses grew passionate. Then he satisfied my hunger for his masculinity, for his strength, for his dominance.

The next morning, he was gone by the time my alarm went off. Abigail had coffee made and I joined her with a smile.

"Good morning," she greeted, herself smiling.

"It is a good morning," I agreed and added, "because of you."

"How so?" she wondered.

I explained how the homework task devoured all my energy and how, last night, I was able to enjoy my children and my husband.

"Your husband," Abigail repeated knowingly.

"Oh, yeah!", I exclaimed nodding. "It's been a long time."

The days continued in this same manner with Abigail's patience and lovingkindness transforming our group into a loving family. When she received her first paycheck, she helped further when she said she didn't need our insurance because she was covered by her husband's plan. This was hundreds of dollars per month that would relieve the stress on Donald. As we thanked her gratefully, she insisted that we thank God; it was his provision, not hers.

# Chapter 5

Years have a way of slipping by making Joanie 16 years old and herself a soccer coach assistant. Abigail and I attended the games, with the boys, now 14 and 13, on their own soccer teams. At one game, the boys were on a different field and, when it was time for Joanie's team to play, I joined her. It had, thankfully, been a long time since I had lusted after Smith Jamison but, to my dismay, he and a tall young man were standing on the sidelines talking to Joanie. I walked up to them and Smith saw me.

"Oh, is this your daughter?" he exclaimed. "She said her last name and I wondered."

"Smith," I greeted tartly and looked at the young man.

Smith put his hand on the young man's arm.

"This is Davis, my son," Smith introduced. "Davis, this is Laura Houston. We used to work together."

Davis nodded with a shy smile.

"Davis is a coach," Joanie added. "His team might be playing against Andrew and Sam."

Joanie looked up at Davis in a way that was unsettling and I was relieved when they left. When Donald got home, I was waiting for him on the deck. Sitting beside me, greeting me with a kiss, he waited, knowing I wanted to talk.

"Smith Davis and his son were talking to Joanie today," I began. "I don't like it."

"At soccer?" he guessed, knowing Joanie had a game.

I nodded and he sighed.

"She's going to be interested in boys," Donald stated. "That's how she's designed."

"How can we protect her from the Smith Jamison's of the world?" I wailed. "One little mistake and her life is ruined."

Donald leaned back looking at Heaven. He was analyzing the situation which I've watched him do many times.

"I remember when I was born-again," he mused. "Do you?"

I nodded; it was a distinct day in my life.

"Because our children aren't born-again, they aren't being led by God," he began, "so we have to lead them. Otherwise, their friends will, their teachers will, or movies, books and all the other secular sources bombarding them. Let's pray."

Donald took my hand.

"Dear Lord, Laura and I are worried about Joanie, Andrew and Sam as they grow into adults. Temptations are everywhere, Lord, begging them to follow those sexual urges that you gave us for the marriage bed. Lead us and guide us, as you said you would do, Lord. Help us. Amen."

Wrapping his arm around my shoulder, I pressed myself against him, absorbing his strength, looking at the night sky with hope that God would hear and answer.

God's answer did come in a wondrous way. Donald, having worked at his job for over twenty years, had invested in the company. When a huge corporation bought the company, Donald received a payout that was enough to pay off the mortgage with a healthy sum left in savings. Though Donald planned to eventually resume working somewhere, he took some time off. It was clear to me that his agenda was to protect, lead and guide Joanie, Andrew and Sam through their teen years.

I was his first project though as he planned a getaway at a luxurious resort where we frolicked like we were newlyweds. After we got home, he made regular 'dates' with Joanie. By his actions, whether he knew it or not, he demonstrated how a godly man behaved and talked. At the soccer fields, he stayed close to Joanie, never letting her talk alone with Davis or other boys.

In the evenings, he gathered us together for Bible study. The children, of course, had all kinds of ideas about the Bible based on what they saw in secular media. He let them challenge him and patiently, consistently presented what he saw in the Bible. He and I prayed for them to be born-again and for their lives to be led by the Holy Spirit.

One afternoon, Abigail got an upsetting call. Her son and his wife, Ethan and Leah, were coming home from India; his wife was ill, probably terminal. A house on our street was for sale and we knew the owners. We asked if they would rent it and they agreed. The day Ethan's flight would arrive, all of us piled into the van to the airport. When Ethan and Leah got off the plane, Leah was in a wheel chair, thin and pale.

Abigail moved in with her son and stayed, even after Leah's death. She eventually bought the house. Ethan immediately got involved in youth ministry and led services that Joanie, Andrew and Sam attended. Ethan was also a soccer fan and got involved with Andrew and Sam's team. Abigail and Ethan became our closest social friends.

When soccer season was over, Donald and I were sitting with the boys in the family room. Joanie, now 17, came in and notified Donald and me that Davis wanted to take her to dinner.

"He's welcome to come here," Donald offered.

Joanie pouted and I braced myself.

"We can't go to a public place and have dinner?" Joanie wailed. "You don't trust me to do that?"

"There are things I don't trust like physical urges and ignorance of God," Donald stated.

"Whose ignoring God?" Joanie challenged.

"Where does Davis go to church?" Donald asked.

"Aaaaghhhh," Joanie cried turning away, stamping her feet. "He'll come to church someday. I'm working on him."

"Good," Donald responded. "Let's talk about it then."

Joanie glared at him, arms crossed. He rose to his full six feet and looked down at her.

"Does anyone want popcorn?" he asked the group, keeping his eyes on her and making his voice a little deeper and louder than usual.

Donald walked past her, letting his arm graze her shoulder to give her a taste of his strength. She stomped out of the room grumbling. I joined him in the kitchen.

"Things might get ugly," he declared. "You up for it?"

"To protect her?" I responded. "Yes, Sir."

"If she won't respect our wishes," he said, "we have to start taking away privileges, OK? Starting with the phone."

Taking some beverages to the family room with the popcorn, we passed Joanie's room and she was wailing to someone on her phone. As he passed the door, Donald informed her that popcorn was ready. Though she didn't join us, he at least invited her. He had no malice toward her behavior; he was protecting her.

A few months later, the Youth Ministry arranged for a Christian rock band to put on a concert. All of us attended, enjoying the praise and worship along with Ethan's message. At the end of the service, Joanie told us she was going home with Ethan. With no reason to believe otherwise, we headed for home. Ethan, while outside saying good night to the band members, saw Joanie get into a waiting sports car. Not recognizing this car and having bad feelings about what he was witnessing, he rushed to his car to follow. He dialed our number. We had not yet reached our house.

"This may sound a little weird, but I'm following Joanie who is in a black sports car," Ethan stated.

"She's not with you?" Donald cried. "She said she was going with you!"

"No, like I said, I saw her get into this car," Ethan repeated.

"Where are you?" Donald demanded and, when Ethan gave him an intersection, Donald responded. "I'm heading that way."

Like we were watching an action movie, all of us were mesmerized.

"I'm at Main and Eighth," Ethan reported. "This is not a good part of town."

"That's an understatement," Donald agreed.

"They are turning right, and I'm behind traffic," Ethan stated and after several seconds, he resumed, "I lost the car."

"Lord, please help us," Donald whispered.

"Amen," I said and so did the boys.

Donald turned right on Main and Eighth and he saw Ethan's car.

"I see your car," Donald reported.

"Do you see that building where the kids are gathered?" Ethan asked.

"I see it," Donald affirmed, "but I don't see Joanie."

# Reboot - Joanie
# Chapter 1

"Da-vis! Da-vis! Da-vis!" cheered some of the guys as Davis walked past, and one of them walked up to him with a smile, "Who is this?"

"Joanie," I said shyly to the man with no shirt and spiky blue hair.

He slowly licked his lips, with a gaze on my chest.

"Are you sharing tonight, Davis?" No-Shirt asked.

"Nah, I'm keeping this for myself," Davis responded.

"I can see why," No-Shirt declared. "She's giving me a hard-on."

Davis laughed.

"Yeah, she's hot," Davis agreed and he bent down close to No-Shirt, "*all* the time. Her body is always begging for it."

At the bar, he pulled out some money and got a six-pack. Then, walking into a hall, he peered into dimly-lit rooms where nude bodies were writhing on mattresses. The air was thick and smelly.

"Where are we going?" I finally asked, not liking what I was seeing.

"We'll find an empty room and have some drinks," Davis stated. "We'll talk, OK?"

Going up a flight of stairs past more rooms, an empty one came into view and we sat in the corner leaning against the wall.

"I thought we were going to a party," I whined. "I thought we would dance."

"We can dance here," Davis promised. "We'll have fun, you'll see."

Opening one of the cans, he handed it to me then he opened his. He pulled two white pills out of his shirt pocket, popped one in his mouth and gulped his drink. He offered me the other pill which I declined.

"Come on," he begged. "You'll like it!"

Turning away, he grabbed the hair on the back of my head. When I gasped, he threw the pill in my mouth then, holding my chin, poured in the drink, spilling it down my shirt. I choked for several seconds.

"Look there, your clothes are messy," he taunted.

Grabbing the hem of my shirt, he started to pull it off, laughing. Pulling on his arms and struggling to get up, he slammed me down against the wall.

"You don't want to leave!" he commanded.

"Take me home!" I wailed as tears flowed down my face.

This abuse was enough to cause tears, but the real pain was realizing that Donald, my dad, was right. This was a bad idea.

"RAAAAAID!" Somebody yelled and naked bodies flew past the door of our room.

Davis loosed a barrage of vulgarities and looked out the window. Grabbing my arm he joined the naked stampede and rushed down some external stairs. Police lights were flashing against the drab buildings. Davis had ahold of my hand along with the rest of his six pack heading toward his car. Struggling to be released from Davis' grip, I wished for an officer to appear in front of us, but, without warning, my head started spinning.

When my eyes opened, I was in a bed in a dark room and I had to use the bathroom. A black shade was blocking the sunlight. Two men were talking outside the door. Pushing back the covers, I gasped to see my naked body with bruises on my breasts, arms and legs. There was an uncomfortable feeling between my thighs. Peering out the black shade, I didn't recognize the neighborhood. As my eyes adjusted, I saw some of my clothes. Not finding my panties, I put on my bra, capris and shirt that smelled like alcohol. Wanting to find my purse and phone, I raised the shade. The walls were covered with skulls, rock bands and naked girls. Trying to open drawers quietly, I found a gun, bottles of pills, knives, a blackjack, handcuffs then I stopped searching as footsteps approached the door. Davis' dad, Smith Jamison, stood in the doorway.

"Good morning," he greeted like all this was perfectly normal. "I hear you partied last night!"

"I need the restroom," I responded softly.

He walked a few steps to a bathroom that was in desperate need of cleaning.

"Do you want some coffee?" he asked when I emerged.

I agreed because it smelled good, though I never had coffee before; I took a sip. It tasted like medicine but it felt good going down. Davis came into the room in his soccer shorts and top.

"Look whose up!" he declared as he sat across from me then he continued, "I guess that pill was too much for you."

"Which pill?" Smith demanded.

Davis gave him a name I didn't recognize.

"Yeah," Smith laughed, "I guess that would be too much for her."

He looked at me.

"Cut it in half, next time," he advised. "Give yourself time to adjust."

"I want to go home," I whined, my face puckering wanting to cry.

"No! No!" Davis protested. "That's not what you said last night. You said you were mine forever."

"I don't remember last night," I wailed. "Please take me home."

"I can't believe you want to go back to those uptight know-it-alls," Smith stated with genuine disbelief. "You want to spend your life going to church and studying the Bible?"

Whether he knew it or not, he was asking a good question. Were those the only choices? Filth like this or Church and Bible Study? Smith got a phone call and went outside.

"You *gave* yourself to me last night," Davis insisted. "You gave yourself to *me*."

"Did I, really?" I challenged, "or did you take it? You gave me a pill. Whatever you did to me, I wasn't a part of it. It's called 'date rape.'"

"I'm telling you, you enjoyed every second," Davis whispered putting his hand on my face.

He squatted beside me. I turned away. Cupping my chin, he brushed his lips on mine and I inhaled involuntarily as lightening shot through my body. There was a throbbing between my legs.

"See there," he exclaimed. "You love it."

Getting up, I headed toward the door but he picked me up and carried me to his room. Holding down my chest, he pulled off my capris, as I kicked at him. He had to let go of me to pull down his pants. Pushing myself up, I jumped off the bed and ran at my fastest soccer speed out the door. Seeing a lady, who gasped at my nudity, I screamed 'call 911'. Davis was catching up with me. Running past her, past other bystanders, I continued to scream 'call 911'. Grasping me from behind, Davis picked me up laughing.

"She's drunk," he explained, smiling, as he carried me toward the house. "She's OK."

Hearing a siren, I screamed 'HELP ME! HE'S RAPING ME!' and thrashed violently trying to loosen his grip. The officer rushed toward me and Davis let me go.

"ON THE GROUND!" the officer bellowed. "ON THE GROUND! ARMS ABOVE YOUR HEAD! LEGS SPREAD!"

To my amazement, he meant me, too, but I gladly complied. We were cuffed. Davis was cursing profusely. Smith rushed to the scene and added to the cursing chorus. Another police car arrive with a female officer. She helped me up and put a blanket on my shoulders.

At the police station, a large room of desks, with phones and computer monitors everywhere, I called my parents.

"JOANIE!" my mom exclaimed. "Thank God! Donald, it's Joanie!"

"Where are you," my dad asked briskly; not angry, but worried.

"At a police station," I answered, "I don't know which one."

Handing the phone to the officer, she gave him the address and said to bring some clothes and shoes. When they asked if I wanted to press charges, I declined. Wanting to be sure I wasn't intimidated, she explained that she would support any charges I wanted to press. I told her that I had gone on the date with him voluntarily and I blamed myself.

It seemed like forever before I heard my parents. They entered the large room, but the female officer took them to another desk. Every time

I glanced at them, one of them or the other was looking at me. Finally, my mom shot up and rushed toward me. Dad was close behind.

"Joanie! Joanie!" my mom wailed with tears streaming, embracing me with all the strength she had.

When she let go, I stood up and faced my dad. He reached for me and I fell into his arms.

"I'm sorry, Dad," I murmured then I stood back to look at him. "You were right. I should have listened to you."

"Let's go home," he replied with a warm smile, rubbing my shoulder.

Mom handed me a bag of clothes and I changed in the ladies' room. I threw the clothes contaminated with alcohol and Davis into the trash.

# Chapter 2

As I walked through the door of my house, I wanted to hug and kiss every piece of furniture, every wall, and the floor, even the clean toilet. What I had taken for granted before was now a cherished treasure. Sitting in my room, I absorbed its wholesomeness and the picture on the wall of flowers with a Bible verse,

"I will praise thee; for I am fearfully and wonderfully made: marvelous are thy works; and that my soul knoweth right well." Psalm 139:14[3]

Hungry, now that I had showered and my body had calmed down, I walked into the kitchen. Mom and Dad were talking on the deck.

"She's not showing any sign of regret," my mom was saying. "It's like nothing happened."

"That doesn't surprise me," my dad replied. "She and the boys have grown up watching shows about rapes, killing, theft - some of it was glorified. I worked with a couple of 'playboy' sales reps who talked about the women they 'dated'. They made a big deal about landing a virgin."

Making a noise so they could hear me, I walked to them with an apple. They made room for me between them as they had a thousand times before. I told my mom I was fine when she asked. The boys were kicking around a soccer ball. Mom commented they were in state finals, which I knew. One of them yelled at me and, handing Mom my apple core, I rushed to join them.

It took another six weeks before the incident impacted me seriously. I missed my period and I knew well what that meant - a baby was growing inside me. Not wanting to tell my parents, I walked to Abigail's house.

"A baby!" she exclaimed with a broad smile, "How wonderful!"

"Wonderful?" I responded. "Will Mom and Dad think it's wonderful?"

"Well," she began, "they won't think it's wonderful that you're not married or that the father is that devil's son."

"Devil's son?" I questioned.

"That Smith Jamison," she answered. "He's a devil."

"How do you know it's Davis?" I wondered.

"Is that his name? Davis?" she replied. "Could it be anyone else?"

I shook my head, looking down then I scoffed.

"I don't even remember what happened," I mused.

"What do you remember?" Abigail pressed gently.

It felt good relaying the entire story.

"Your parents caused that raid, you know!" Abigail declared.

"How?" I exclaimed.

"Ethan saw you leave in that black sports car and he followed you," Abigail began. "He called your dad. When they got to the building, they called 911."

"Oh! My! God!" I blurted.

"They even went to that devil's house, assuming it was Davis that you went with," Abigail recounted. "That devil told them you weren't there. He even invited them inside and led them to Davis who denied knowing where you were."

"I was passed out in his bed," I wailed leaning back in my chair and looking to Heaven."Why would God let this happen to me or...to them. They love God!"

"God didn't create robots," Abigail explained. "You were given instructions to follow and you chose your own way. Our actions result in consequences."

Anger rose in me.

"Don't be getting mad at me, Young Lady, or your parents or God!" Abigail exclaimed. "You made your bed and now you have to lie in it. Get home now and tell your parents and the father."

As I walked back to my house, Davis' black sports car was in my driveway. I felt sick. Looking back toward Abigail's, her command to 'get home' pushed me to go on. Davis, Smith and my parents were sitting at the kitchen table.

"Here she is," my dad stated.

Everyone looked at me.

"Here she is," Smith repeated patting Davis' shoulder. "Davis has a question for you."

Davis pulled out a small black box and got on one knee. He was trembling. I felt like throwing up.

"Joanie," he began looking at me with puppy eyes, "I'm sorry if I hurt you. I went about this the wrong way, but this was my intention all along. Will you marry me?"

Putting my shirt on my mouth, I gagged and ran into the bathroom.

"Joanie!" my mom yelled, following me.

She closed the door and gently rubbed my back as the spasms forced gunk out of my stomach. Mom turned on the hot water and soaked a wash cloth. When my body calmed down, I sat on the edge of the tub and held the warm cloth to my face. She sat on the toilet watching me intently.

"I'm pregnant," I revealed looking at her, more concerned about her than myself. "I'm sorry, Mom."

Her face puckered and she looked to Heaven letting tears fall.

"Regardless of the circumstances, it's a gift from God," she consoled. "It's something to be thankful for and cherish."

For the first time ever, smelling like puke, sitting in a bathroom, I felt a warm glow. Though I wanted it to last forever, I knew I had to tell Davis. Mom got me some clean clothes as I washed my chest and arms. We walked back to the kitchen.

"Was that a 'no'?" Smith quipped.

That made me laugh and others followed.

"I'm pregnant," I stated flatly, just wanting to get it out.

My dad stood up and pulled me close, embracing me tightly. It strengthened me. When he released me, Davis was looking at his dad.

"I'll pay for the abortion," Smith announced, like he was a hero.

The room became deathly still and both my parents looked at me.

"I'll have the baby," I offered like it was something to be negotiated.

"They're too young for this much responsibility," Smith argued, looking at Donald. "It will be a financial burden."

My mom and dad remained quiet. It was my choice and they were making me choose. Davis was letting his dad talk.

"What about college?" Smith continued. "Davis has another two years! And he's talking about a masters."

I took Davis' hand and led him to the back yard. He reached for me and I stepped away from him.

"This is happening too fast," I began. "I'm not killing the baby."

"But my dad..." Davis whined.

"It's not his decision," I retorted. "You obviously aren't ready for marriage and fatherhood. Let's wait until you're ready, OK?"

He reached for me and I again backed away.

"Davis!" I blurted. "All you know is sex. For some reason, you crave sex from me. Can you explain that?"

He looked at me, silent, lost. Compassion rose in me.

"If you truly love me, you can see me at church," I offered. "I'll meet you at church every Sunday and we can have dinner here."

He didn't agree or disagree. I walked away from him and he followed. In the house, he told his dad he wanted to leave.

On Saturday night, Davis called wanting to see me. Reminding him of my proposal, I gave him the address of the church. On Sunday, he met us next to the marquee. During the service, I let him hold my hand. At home, Abigail and Ethan joined us for dinner.

My dad engaged Davis with soccer and sports talk. Davis stated that he planned to get his masters in physical education. He went on to explain that a masters might lead to a coaching job hopefully with a professional soccer team where the big money is. Ethan talked about a young soccer player who recently had a born-again experience. I asked Ethan what that meant.

"It's a second birth," Ethan began. "The first birth is your body or your 'flesh' and the second birth is your spirit."[4]

"Doesn't everyone have a second birth?" I asked.

"You have to choose," Ethan and Andrew said at the same time.

Most of us laughed. Davis was concentrating on his food. Ethan let Andrew continue.

"God wants us to choose him," Andrew explained. "If we choose him sincerely, we will follow Jesus by reading the Bible and praying."

"Are you born-again?" I asked Andrew.

"I am," he responded. "It happened about a year ago at Ethan's service."

Andrew smiled and pushed Ethan who laughed.

"That was a great night," Ethan declared, beaming.

The contrast between Davis and Ethan was striking. Davis, bending over his food, was not looking at anyone while Ethan was smiling, glowing, engaging. Explaining to myself that Davis didn't know us very well, I let it go.

When Davis was done eating he rose to leave. Following him to the door, he took my hand and led me to the car.

"Let's go for a ride," he pleaded.

I backed away.

"I'll see you next Sunday," I replied and tried to loosen his grip on my hand.

He opened the passenger door. I backed away with all my strength.

"You're killing me!" he cried then he yanked me close. "You want it as much as I do."

"Joanie," Abigail called, coming out of the house with Ethan. "I knitted some things for the baby."

Turning away from Davis, I joined Abigail and Ethan. Davis passed us, squealing his tires.

# Chapter 3

Although Davis attended church sporadically, he and Smith showed up at the hospital when Mom called them. When asked, he obediently posed for pictures with the baby, Caitlin, and me. On the day of my release from the hospital, Davis, evidently thinking he had passed the test, assumed, along with Smith, I was going to his house to live.

"Mom is going to babysit while I work," I announced. "But I have to get my GED[5]."

"Why go through that crap?" Smith challenged. "Davis can get welfare until he starts working."

Seeing that they were sensing 'free money' for the next five years while Davis studied for his masters and, probably assuming I would cook and clean for them, I refused to comply.

"I'm not waiting for you forever!" Davis bellowed. "There are plenty of girls who want me!"

Thankfully, Mom and Dad showed up. They invited Smith and Davis to the house but they declined. Abigail and Ethan joined us for dinner and both lavished their attention on Caitlin. Abigail made it known she was available to babysit any time.

The next Sunday, Davis showed up at church and he followed us home but he didn't stay for dinner. He wanted to talk and I led him to the deck.

"I have my rights as a father," he began. "I want visitation."

"Are you paying support?" I challenged.

"How the hell can I pay support?" he bellowed. "I'm at school all day and coaching at night."

"Caitlin has the right to be supported," I answered flatly.

He stood up and started pacing.

"You're putting me through hell!" he raged. "All of this is about YOU!"

"You're demonstrating right now that you aren't a fit father," I observed. "I'm not exposing her to your temper and bad judgment."

He leaned down with his hands on the back of the chair.

"All you have to do is let me F-you," he hissed. "Is that too much to ask?"

"You can see Caitlin at church and at Sunday dinner," I answered, rising.

He wrapped his arms around me and mouthed my lips. My body reacted just like he knew it would as a groan escaped and my knees went weak responding to my pulsing groin.

"What is wrong with you?" he whispered. "I could strip you and take you right here and you know it."

He had physical evidence to support what he claimed. I didn't have a verbal argument to present. I pushed him back and he relented.

"There's more than F-you!" I cried.

Tired of the debate, I escaped into the house and closed the door to my room. His tires squealed as he left.

The next round was with Smith who showed up later that afternoon. Thankfully I was nursing and Mom came into the nursery.

"Smith is here," Mom announced.

"Dear, Lord," I cried looking to Heaven then explained to my mom. "They want visitation rights."

"They can visit on Sunday," she repeated the agreement we all had made.

"I told Davis that today," I responded. "But he doesn't really care about Caitlin. He just wants his way with me."

"Let me get your dad," she suggested and left the room.

Dad came in.

"Your mother said they want visitation rights," Dad began then continued. "Let's suggest counseling sessions."

"That's what he needs," I agreed wholeheartedly.

"For both of you," he added.

I sighed and agreed.

"Would you be comfortable with Ethan as counselor?" Dad asked.

I nodded and thanked God that my dad went to talk to Smith. It wasn't a friendly exchange, as one would expect. Dad returned to the nursery and Mom joined him. He got on speaker phone with Ethan.

"Hey there," Ethan greeted. "I'm with my mom."

"Hi, Abigail," Mom and I greeted back.

Dad muted the phone and looked at me.

"Do you want Abigail to leave?" he asked.

I shook my head, welcoming her participation.

"I'm calling about Joanie and Davis," Dad said. "Can we set up counseling sessions for them?"

"Yes, of course," Ethan answered. "But I need them to contact me."

"No problem, Ethan," I joined in. "Caitlin and I are here."

"Can I come over and we can discuss further?" Ethan suggested.

At the appointed time, Ethan showed up and I led him to the deck with some iced tea. After I described today's episode, he asked what I wanted.

"I want a home like this," I stated, lifting my arm to indicate my house.

"How would you describe that?" he asked.

I searched for adjectives.

"Clean, safe," I began still searching, "satisfying."

"That's a good start," Ethan said. "All of that takes decision and effort, yes? If you decide not to dust, your furniture will be dusty."

"So true," I giggled.

"What is your definition of sin?" Ethan probed.

"Sin is doing bad things," I answered simply.

"Who decides what is bad?" Ethan pressed.

"God does?" I questioned.

"You're saying 'God does' but do you believe it?" Ethan challenged.

"If God doesn't decide then we do, I guess," I responded, "but I would never accept Davis' definition of sin."

"I'm glad you realize that, because, if we each define sin, there will be a million definitions," Ethan explained. "So, I think a good starting point is for you and Davis to agree on a definition of sin. How's that?"

I nodded and smiled. Talking to Ethan made me feel safe; I was looking forward to the sessions.

# Chapter 4

Davis called me to complain about the counseling sessions.

"I don't have time for this crap!" Davis raged. "Call it off!"

"This is proof to me that you don't love me," I responded.

"Do *you* love *me*?" he countered. "I know women who would die for me."

"Crazy women," I declared. "Sick, ignorant women."

He ended the call.

At the first counseling session at the church, Davis didn't show up and Ethan cancelled it. He said it would not be appropriate for us to be meeting alone. When I asked why, he laughed.

"I'm a man and you're a woman," he explained. "It's a powerful combination, and, as you have discovered, it should be handled carefully."

Davis didn't come to Sunday service nor did he show up for the second session. Wanting to talk more with Ethan, I wondered if Abigail could join us. Ethan agreed and we met at his house.

In Abigail's dining room, the three of us began the session with prayer.

"When we talked last, we decided to define sin," Ethan stated. "Did you decide on a definition of sin?"

"I have decided sin is whatever God says it is," I responded.

"Have you broken any of the ten commandments?" Ethan asked.

"I would say I have broken all of them," I admitted glibly.

"So have I," Ethan also admitted and Abigail admitted the same.

"You know where this is going, don't you?" he stated.

"Jesus died for my sins," I repeated, "but, I've heard that hundreds of times and it doesn't affect me like it affects you and Abigail."

"This is a good stopping point," Ethan decided. "Will you say to God what you just said to me? Let's see if he answers."

At home, when I got to my room, I knelt.

"God," I started, "I know Jesus died for my sins but something is missing. I see it in Abigail and Ethan. Will you help me?"

That night, Andrew, now assistant coach, was going to a soccer game. Asking me to drive him, I was happy to oblige. With Caitlin in a stroller, it felt good to be on the sidelines again cheering the team. Davis was on the other side of the field in a lawn chair with a girl sitting next to him. Whether or not it was for my benefit, I don't know, but he leaned over and kissed her passionately while putting his hand up her shirt. Turning away, I walked to the other end of the field. It wasn't jealousy, it was aversion. Something in me said that sex is not a public activity and yet, Davis took me to that place where sex was being performed in all of those rooms. Then, when No-Shirt asked Davis if he was 'sharing', I realized that Davis could have agreed to share me with that man or any man in that place. Finally, I realized that Davis had sex with me without my permission. He didn't even need me to be conscious. Clearly, Davis places no value on women.

After the game, Davis' car was parked at the house when Andrew and I pulled in. He was talking with my Dad at the kitchen table. With dread, I walked to the kitchen; Dad excused himself and went to the family room.

"I saw you at the soccer field and realized how much I missed you," Davis stated. "I want to see you."

"No," I responded flatly. "It's over, Davis."

"That girl is nobody," he explained, rolling his eyes. "They're a dime a dozen."

"It's not the girl," I responded. "Listen to me: I'm an 'experience' that you especially like with the same status as a drug or a dessert. You don't see me or any woman as a person. You have no clue what a relationship is."

"I DON'T KNOW WHAT YOU WANT FROM ME!" he bellowed, pounding the table so hard the chandelier rattled.

"You can see me at church," I responded. You can see me at counseling sessions. If you want visitation rights, I'll see you in court."

I stood up and waited for him to get up. He glared at me.

"Dad!" I yelled and he appeared immediately then I turned to Davis. "You aren't welcome here, anymore, Davis."

He rose slowly from the table and walked just as slowly to the door. He deliberately knocked a table lamp off the table. His tires screeched as he left. Turning to my dad, I wrapped my arms around him.

"I'm sorry, Dad," I said into his shirt, which muffled my voice. "If I had listened to you..."

"You're paying a huge price for a valuable lesson," he replied, pulling me close. "The only pain I feel is watching you suffer. But, Joanie, God forgives you, so I forgive you."

At the next counseling session with Abigail and Ethan, I informed them that Davis would probably not be participating but I did pray about what I was feeling.

"I don't think God answered yet," I said.

"That's OK," Ethan responded. "He will answer when it's time."

"What if I died on the way home?" I quipped, only half serious.

"He's aware of what's going to happen," Ethan replied. "He knows your heart."

"So, Smith, of all people, asked me a question once," I remembered. "I was at their house which was a horrible place. Smith asked me if I wanted to stay with Davis or go back to Church and Bible study. Are those the only choices? Can't we choose a place in between?"

"Remember last time, we agreed that everyone would break the ten commandments?" Ethan started. "So there are always going to be liars, thieves, adulterers, killers, and so on."

"I remember," I stated. "Can't we create a place that is 'neutral' "?

"We can't escape sin, Joanie!" Ethan cried, showing unusual frustration. "I think that's what you're not getting. When Adam and Eve disobeyed God, sin *entered the world*, Romans 5:12[6] then King David declared he was '*born in sin*' in Psalms 51:5.[7] More importantly, God created everything. Everything! You're asking him to walk away from it. It's like saying, 'Joanie, walk away from your baby.' "

"*That* I can relate to," I declared.

"These are the facts," Ethan stated. "First, we can't escape sin. Second, God destroys sin with his wrath.[8] Third, God poured out his wrath on Jesus.[9] Finally, we must reach out to Jesus and pledge allegiance to him. I know the Bible says 'believe', but Jesus isn't Santa Claus. We must follow him then he will renew our spirits and we will be led and guided by the Holy Spirit.[10] It's not complicated. The answer is 'yes' or 'no'. 'Life or 'death'. 'Good or evil.'"

Ethan not only ended today's session but the counseling sessions. He told me to read the Bible and pray.

Walking home, Davis' car was parked in front of my house. He must have seen me because the car moved slowly in my direction. Sprinting back to Abigail's, Davis bellowed at me to get in the car. A shot was fired and I screamed with terror. Ethan rushed to the porch; another shot was fired and Ethan went down. I crawled to Ethan and covered him with my body. One more shot blew out a window. Sirens were blaring. Davis pulled away screeching his tires.

Abigail, on the phone with 911, knelt beside Ethan and me. My mom and dad arrived breathless. The medic pulled me off and blood gushed out of Ethan's chest. Pulling a gauze out of his bag, he immediately applied pressure. They got him into the squad. I told them I was alright when they asked. Each of us reported to the police officers what we saw. All of us were anxious to get to the hospital.

In the waiting room, we were told that Ethan was in surgery. Hours later a doctor came out and he asked for Abigail.

"Chances are good your son will recover," the doctor reported. "He's young and healthy. He didn't lose as much blood as he could have. Your first aid probably saved his life."

"First aid?" my mom wondered after the doctor left.

"It was you, Joanie," Abigail stated. "You laid on him. Your body applied pressure to the wound."

"I...I just wanted to protect him," I answered softly.

# Chapter 5

It was a week before Ethan was allowed visitors. Abigail escorted me up to see him; he smiled instantly when I entered the room.

"Hi there," he greeted. "How are you and Caitlin?"

"The bigger question is 'how are you?' " I countered.

"I'm blessed," he answered, "and will be leaving soon. Hallelujah!"

Abigail and I laughed. Then Ethan looked at me with softness in his eyes.

"You put yourself between me and danger," Ethan stated quietly. "You essentially laid down your life for me."

That flustered me and I didn't know what to say. I didn't plan it; it just happened. He winced slightly as he leaned forward to take my hand.

"Thank you," he continued. "I will thank you forever."

Though he wasn't near me, I felt like he was caressing me. A soft, peaceful glow engulfed me. For hours, we talked and greeted visitors as they came and went. Finally, seeing that Ethan was getting tired, Abigail and I said 'good-night'. I didn't want to leave him.

On the drive home, Abigail said she would have a dinner party when Ethan felt like it. So many people worried about him. She asked about Davis and I told her he was arrested and he pled guilty for a five year sentence.

"Do you think I should visit him?" I asked Abigail.

"You might visit him as a ministry," Abigail responded with a distressed look, "but, as I understand it, he needs to change, right? Even if he doesn't follow Jesus, he has to change?"

"For sure," I agreed wholeheartedly. "You're right. I can't visit him as a girlfriend or even the mother of his child."

"Ethan will visit him," Abigail stated with confidence.

"Really?" I marveled. "Davis shot Ethan and Ethan will visit him?"

"Ethan is very aware that the sin nature drives people," Abigail explained. "He focuses on the poor suffering soul under the sin."

"Does he do that to me?" I ventured to ask.

Abigail smiled and chuckled.

"He does it to everyone," she repeated, not looking at me.

I felt like she was keeping a secret.

Abigail did have her dinner party at the church. Ethan, looking better than ever, spoke a few words of thanks for everyone's concern. Filling our plates from a buffet, Abigail sat Ethan at the head of the table and she beckoned me to sit beside her. I caught Ethan glancing at me more than once.

A few months later, it was my nineteenth birthday and I had been awarded my GED so Mom invited Ethan and Abigail to Sunday dinner. Caitlin was sitting up on her own and was center stage. She smiled widely every time Ethan said anything to her. Sitting across from Ethan and Abigail, both glanced at me in a way I thought was unusual. I decided to find out from Abigail what was going on.

A few days later when I knew Ethan was away from home, Caitlin and I walked to Abigail's. In her favorite chair, knitting, she was delighted to be able to hold Caitlin.

"Ethan looks like he's nearly normal," I began. "Any after-effects?"

"He does get headaches now," Abigail replied. "The doctor says it is common."

"Did it scar badly?" I asked.

"There is a puncture scar and some suture scars," Abigail replied, looking at me intently. "Is there a reason for your visit?"

"Is there?" I retorted.

She chuckled and looked to Heaven.

"Lord, help me," she sighed, closing her eyes then she looked at me. "Ethan is interested in you."

"Oh, wow!" I blurted leaning back in my chair.

Though I had wondered if Ethan was interested, the verbal affirmation had an impact.

"Is that a good 'wow' or a bad one?" Abigail impishly asked.

"It's an unbelievable 'wow,'" I replied. "How could he be interested in me? How could I possibly measure up to him?"

Abigail laid back in her chair chuckling.

"I shouldn't tell you this," she stated and looked at me. "He was in agony when he saw what Davis was doing to you. I comforted him many times as he wept for you."

This was unfathomable to me. Thinking of the women at church who would qualify as a wife for him, I was dumbstruck. The front door opened and Ethan walked in. I gasped.

"Ladies," he greeted, smiling, then he bent down to coo at Caitlin.

"I saw Davis," Ethan reported. "He's having a hard time."

I nodded, staring at him. Ethan seemed to notice my stare.

"What's going on?" he asked looking at Abigail then back at me.

"It's time for honesty," Abigail replied getting up and taking Caitlin into the kitchen.

We looked at each other. He looked at me with that soft caress; I suppose I was looking at him with wonder.

"What did she tell you?" Ethan began.

"She said you're interested in me," I answered flatly.

An involuntary laugh escaped and he blushed.

"I sensed it, Ethan. Should I have come to you?" I asked.

"I..I don't know. I'm glad you know," Ethan stuttered. "Wait! You sensed it?"

I nodded, starting to feel giddy at his confusion.

"Dear, Lord," he cried looking to Heaven. "There will be no secrets from Joanie!"

He squatted so he could talk to me face-to-face.

"So I was thinking I would ask your parents about taking you to dinner," he stated.

"My parents?" I challenged. "I'm 19, with a child."

"True, but I'm thirteen years older," he reasoned. "I can't have them upset with me. You know, 'honor your parents'? My plan was, if they object, to wait until they were comfortable."

"I'm pretty sure they won't object," I smiled wanting to touch him.

"Joanie," he said seriously, "I want to go back to India. Think about that, will you? Pray about it. I've got some pictures to show you. It's a tough life."

# Reboot - Caitlin
# Chapter 1

The plane landed and I was in America for the first time. Following signs to luggage pickup, a woman held a poster, "Welcome Caitlin Lindsay". Nodding and waving at her, she rushed toward me with arms extended. I let her hug me; she was so excited.

"I'm your Grandma Laura and this is Grandpa Donald," Laura began then she turned to the other two men. "These are your uncles, Andrew and Sam."

All of them hugged me.

"How was the trip?" Laura asked. "Are you hungry?"

"I'm tired," I answered. "I got on the plane day before yesterday."

Walking into my grandparents' house, I was greeted with pictures of my parents and me at various ages. Mom's room was just like I pictured: comfortable and clean. Thanking God for a safe trip, I welcomed sleep.

The next day, my dad's mother, Abigail, visited along with Andrew and Sam, still bachelors and renting rooms in Abigail's house. They were running their own business, a bookstore on campus. They claimed the books sold themselves as well as the official college gear and there wasn't much competition. The hardest part of the job was managing inventory and taxes. Asking them questions about their software, it was obvious they were years behind.

"I would imagine that kind of software requires a lot of manual input," I guessed.

"It does," Andrew answered with wonder. "Don't they all?"

"It can be cut down with proper setup," I advised.

"Didn't you live in India?" Sam asked. "I'm surprised they can afford computers."

"Many people live in poverty, same as America," I responded, "but many are very intelligent and computer systems are easy for them. I had the best teachers."

"Could you look at our setup?" Andrew suggested.

"She needs a part time job," Laura stated.

The next day, I visited their store and immediately saw displays that I would reorganize. Looking at their system, I knew with a little effort, I could reduce the amount of manual work. Just to show them, I made one change that blew them away. I was hired.

In a few weeks, I was attending college and basically running the store. The boys spent their time helping the droves of students constantly roaming the merchandise tables and stacks. Seeing the healthy operating income produced at the end of my first month, I suggested they hire at least one student helper. Although they were a little nervous, they gave it a try. After another month, they found themselves having time to socialize.

To celebrate, Andrew took me to a professional soccer game. He explained the city had the stadium built a few years ago and that my father was a driving force in the project.

"My *biological* father, you mean?" I asked with some trepidation, remembering the one picture I had of him when I was a newborn.

"Oh, yes, Davis Jamison," he answered.

"What do you know about him?" I pressed.

"I know bits and pieces," Andrew replied. "You should ask your Grandma Laura or Abigail...or both."

Although attending college in America was my main reason for coming, I did want to know about my biological father. My mother, who was adopted, understood perfectly this desire. She remembered visiting the graves of her real parents who had died in a tragic accident. When the opportunity arose, I asked Laura about Davis Jamison. She looked at me with worry.

"Let me start with facts," Laura began. "He raped your mother. He shot at her. He shot your father. He went to prison for five years. He got his masters in prison, got soccer coaching jobs and worked his way up into the top ranks of a soccer league. He makes it into National News some times."

"And your opinion?" I prompted.

"I don't trust him. I never heard that he accepted Jesus, though I wish he would," Laura finished.

"Should I try to see him?" I asked.

"Please, be careful if you do," Laura answered with concern.

In my prayers that night, I asked God what he thought about my visiting Davis Jamison. I told God I would follow his lead.

A month or so later, in a news report about soccer, Davis was filmed coming out of a building. Taking a picture of it, I asked Andrew and Sam where it was. When they didn't know, I asked the student helper. Giving me his best guess, I drove there at the next opportunity.

Parking outside the building where Davis was videoed, I found his name on a marquee. Room C, floor 3. The decor was modern, luxurious, everything based on soccer. Though few people were in the hall, some men were in upscale suits, a few in soccer uniforms and women in designer outfits. Arriving at floor 3, I saw room C, but I was afraid to go in.

The door burst open and Davis rushed briskly past me, a young woman following. She was recording whatever he was saying then they disappeared into an elevator. Another younger man came out, in jeans and tee shirt. Short red hair, slightly spiked, fair skin with freckles, sweet smile, solid muscle and long soccer thighs showing under his jeans. I looked up at him.

"Do you need help?" he asked with concern.

"I...I was here to see Davis Jamison, but I see he left," I stammered.

"Oh, I'm meeting with him in a minute," he offered. "I can tell him you're here."

"Thank you," I responded, looking down, getting cold feet. "I can come back."

"Well, what's your name?" he continued. "Mine is Jackson."

"Caitlin, just tell him Caitlin," I replied and rushed toward the stairs.

Later that week, Laura got a call from Davis and she brought me her phone.

"Caitlin! I heard you visited," Davis exclaimed. "Next time, come in! I'll make time for you. I'll tell my secretary to watch out for you."

He ended the call.

It took a few weeks for me to have time and the courage to go back to Davis' office. Arriving at room C, I opened the door. A young woman, seated at a desk took my name. She punched a few numbers and stated I was in the lobby. In front of me were cubicle walls that formed a hallway to a room of glass overlooking the city. Another young woman approached me.

"Caitlin?" she asked in a sweet southern drawl and she motioned for me to follow her.

We passed the glass room and came to a corner office where she paused and motioned me to go in. I stood in the doorway until Davis saw me.

"Come in, Caitlin," he greeted as he got up and started walking to a couch under a massive window.

When we were seated, he put his arm on the back of the couch and looked at me with wonder. I mean, he looked at me up...and...down.

"Quite a young lady, aren't you," he murmured with a smile then chuckled. "Not surprising. Your mother was one-of-a-kind. She got me in a lot of trouble, you know."

Not knowing how to respond to that, I cleared my throat.

"I wanted to meet you," I stammered.

"Understandable," Davis agreed, nodding. "We should know each other."

His phone rang and he stood up, looking out the window. When he ended the call, he turned back to me.

"I'm having a party tonight," Davis stated. "Can you come? We'll have time to talk. I'm sending you the address from my phone. Come any time after 6:00; food will be served at 8:00.

My phone dinged as his contact appeared then he disappeared out of his office door. Having no idea what to wear, I looked for the lady with the southern drawl, Marybeth, and found her in the first cubicle door. Pulling out her phone with pictures of his past parties, the dresses were low cut, sleeveless, and sparkling. I called Laura and she told me which thrift shop to go to.

Choices at the thrift shop were pretty good; the problem was finding one that fit and I wanted it to be cleaned. Being 4:00 already, I decided to wear one of my Indian saris. Rushing home, I showered, braided my hair and got to Davis' house about 7:00. His estate was impressive and he had a parking valet. The main entrance led to a courtyard with a floor-to-ceiling fountain. The next area was a dining room, I guess, but it was massive, like a hotel party room. Giant screens hung on every wall.

Someone I would call a butler greeted me. Telling him my name, he led me to a table next to a portable stage. Two couples were already seated, the men in upscale suits and the ladies in sparkling gowns. One of the ladies complimented my outfit, asking where I got it. It was surprising to her that I actually got it in India.

Davis appeared with a young woman whose dress was showing practically everything.

"Here is my Indian daughter," Davis laughed, indicating me.

"I'm American but in an Indian sari," I corrected.

The ladies were curious to know about my living in India and why I was now in America. Mentioning college sparked them talking about their sons and daughters. I didn't think much about the empty seat until Jackson joined us in a nice-fitting suit. The conversation then turned to him and his position as team captain and his chances of winning the national championship. Davis and the young woman went on stage and Jackson moved next to me.

"Caitlin?" he guessed.

"Right," I giggled nervously, flattered that he would talk to me.

"Your Davis' daughter?" he ventured further.

"Right," I repeated.

"But you didn't grow up with him?" he continued.

To stop the guessing game, I told him that my mom married a missionary and we lived in India. In addition, I told him I was attending school and working with my uncles at the college bookstore. As these conversations usually do, he asked if I was seeing anyone and wanted to take me to dinner. When I said he was welcome to come to Sunday dinner, he, not surprisingly, lost interest, and he left the table. After dinner was served and Davis didn't come back, I went to find my car and went home. I thought that was all there was to Davis Jamison.

# Chapter 2

A few months later, Laura got a call from Marybeth that Davis was in the hospital recovering from a heart attack. When I expressed uncertainty about visiting him, Laura called Abigail who said she would visit to minister to him and I could come along.

Davis was under intensive care and we weren't allowed to see him. Abigail left a card and we both signed it. A week later, Davis called me inviting me to visit him at home. He told me to drive to the back of the house. When I saw the back entrance, I understood his reason. The entrance was less grand, though elegant, and looked more like a home. Walking into a large foyer, a cozy sitting room with fireplace was on the left, a hallway leading to a back entrance, and a beautiful curved staircase on the right. A gentleman met me and led me up the stairs.

In Davis' room, he was hooked up to a couple of monitors and a nurse was measuring vitals. He noticed me as I entered.

"Oh, my god!" Davis blurted. "It's Joanie!"

"You know I'm not Joanie," I laughed.

"You may as well be!" he cried.

He stared at me, again, up and down.

"I would have loved to see her hair long like yours," he stated rather softly, like he might actually love her.

"And there's Jackson!" he shouted.

Jackson entered the room, smiling large, in a soccer uniform complete with knee high socks. Strolling up to the nurse, he grasped Davis' hand.

"You met Caitlin, right? At the party?" Davis asked. "Hey, you should take her out; show her the hot spots."

"Turned me down flat," Jackson replied, shaking his head.

"That's not exactly true," I intervened and looked at Jackson. "You're welcome to come to Sunday dinner."

"Oh, no!" Davis cried. "Not that crap!"

I was willing to drop the subject.

"This man makes millions of dollars a year!" Davis exclaimed. "You're gonna pass that up?"

"I better go," I stated and turned to leave.

Walking down the hall, I heard Davis ranting about my mom and what *she* did to *him*. As I drove on the long private lane that led to the street, I saw Jackson running after me at soccer speed. I stopped.

"Hey!" he exclaimed, "you shouldn't treat him like that!"

"Treat him like what?" I asked with wonder.

"He's just being nice," Jackson responded. "He's done a lot for me."

"He was badgering me," I stated. "He should respect my wishes. In fact, as my father, he should want to protect me."

"Protect you from what?" Jackson cried.

"From guys who won't come to Sunday dinner," I answered with a smile. "It's an open invitation."

Driving off, he watched me for a while then jogged back to the house. A few days later, Jackson came to the store and Andrew brought him to me. My desk was on a loft, facing a wall. Most people wouldn't look up to see me sitting there. Jackson stood next to the chair then kneeled so he could see me face-to-face.

"Hey," he said softly. "About the other day..."

Then, like a well-executed soccer move, he bent forward, gently wrapped his hand around my neck and brushed his lips on mine. Inhaling involuntarily with an unknown throbbing between my legs, I pushed him away. He looked at me intently.

"Your dad was right," he marveled. "Your body wants it...badly."

"I want you to leave," I demanded, but he continued to stare at me like he was under a spell.

"I can scream and get you in a lot of trouble," I threatened. "The Nightly News would love it."

That seemed to get his attention and he rose quickly but he backed away slowly.

"What time is Sunday dinner?" he asked.

Donald and the boys were mesmerized when Jackson walked through the door, and I felt slightly sorry for him as they gushed their praises of him and the team. My preparations for Jackson's visit included a prayer for protection, wisdom, self-control and obedience to God's will, and I very diligently, with Laura's advice, chose an outfit that was not sexual in any way.

Jackson raved about the food stating it reminded him of dinners at home. When the meal was over, the men watched the sports channel and Laura, Abigail and I sat outside. This was working out well. When we heard the men coming into the living room, we rose to join them. Jackson thanked us and looked at me pointedly, maybe thinking I would follow him to the car. I clung to Donald's arm; he patted my hand, looking at me with a smile. I had told Laura about Jackson's kiss; I also told her I wanted to be a virgin on my wedding night.

When soccer season started, Jackson got Donald and the boys box seats at a home game and they were exploding with excitement. It didn't seem to bother anyone that Davis was the host. Both Laura, Abigail and I knew it was Davis and Jackson trying to get to me.

One Saturday, I was watering flowers in the back yard in shorts and a tank top, not expecting visitors, and the water hose got twisted. Straddling the hose, I bent at the waist to untwist it and I felt hands on my hips and rubbing on my buttocks. Spinning around, it was Jackson in a soccer outfit.

"What are you doing!" I cried, backing away from him.

"Checking the fit," he smiled looking at my crotch, stepping toward me.

"What fit..." then looking at his crotch, I figured it out. "Aaaaghhhh, your despicable! GRANDPA!"

At that moment, the hose untwisted itself and water shot above us. He grabbed the hose and started spraying me. Screaming, I stupidly tried to take it from him then noticed my breasts, with cold nipples protruding, were clearly visible under the wet shirt. Running toward the house, I slipped and landed sideways on my ankle. I heard it snap and howled in pain. Rushing to me, Jackson carried me to a chair on the deck, squatted before me and propped my leg on his knee.

"It's broken," he announced as my leg swelled twice its normal size.

"Where is Grandpa?" I wailed, sobbing in pain and embarrassment.

Jackson rushed into the house and Donald came out asking what happened with Laura following.

"It's broken," Jackson repeated, "I've seen broken ankles a hundred times. I'll take her to the hospital."

"No!" I cried. "Grandpa will take me! I need to change clothes."

"Thank you for stopping by, Jackson," Laura cooed as she gently directed him to the front door.

Though I was furious with him for assaulting me, I noticed he was upset with concern.

In one of the emergency rooms, waiting on x-ray results, I was alone with Donald for a few minutes.

"How did Jackson get in the house?" I asked.

"I let him in," Donald admitted innocently.

"And you left me alone with him?" I challenged.

"What's he gonna do?" Donald retorted glibly.

"How about rubbing his crotch on my buttocks?" I blurted with my face reddening at those intimate words.

Donald grimaced.

"Really?" he replied in disbelief.

"Are you giving him a pass because he's famous?" I accused with raised voice. "Didn't you protect my mom?"

Donald looked down for several seconds.

"You're right," Donald admitted then looked at me intently. "Thank you for reminding me. Your Mom and Dad taught you well."

"They would be praising God for that," I answered.

# Chapter 3

The following Monday, with my leg in a boot to support my ankle, Sam notified Andrew and me that he accepted a job at the soccer league office. When he told us the salary, neither of us could blame him. Andrew and I wished him well and posted a 'help wanted' sign.

When the winter quarter ended, we knew business in the store would fall off during the summer and we talked about an online store, which meant we would need to hire someone to pack and ship. In our estimation, because the software was user friendly, the main qualifications were dedication and honesty.

A few months later, Sam called me about helping him with the software at his marketing office. Thinking nothing of it, I drove to meet him expecting him to stay with me while I analyzed the setup. By the time I got there, everyone had gone home. His office was one of many along the wall of a huge room of cubicles. The wall separating him from the cubicles was made of glass. After about 20 minutes he excused himself then, a few seconds later, Jackson was standing in the doorway. He wanted to show me something and I assumed he was taking me to wherever Sam had gone.

Jackson took two steps outside the door and waited for me to join him; as I walked toward him, I saw Sam leave the huge room under an 'exit' sign. I was two steps from the office door and, instead of going through it, I shut it and locked it.

"What the hell?" Jackson bellowed with an incredulous look. "I just want to talk to you!"

"Call me," I said pulling out my phone as I sat in Sam's chair.

"What the hell?" he repeated on the phone. "I can't even call you a cold bitch because you are the hottest one I ever met!"

"Don't call me names," I demanded and I hung up. I called my Grandpa to come get me.

He mouthed 'sorry'. Then, with his arms above his head, he squished his face into the glass which was hilarious. When he saw he left face prints, he made a row of them. I couldn't suppress laughter.

"You're staying in there all night," he threatened.

"I thought you wanted to talk," I reminded him.

"Can't I take you to dinner?" he begged, then he got on his knees in an imploring position.

"You know the answer," I stated, smiling at him. "In fact, you should probably start coming to church."

He mouthed 'Oh my god' and fainted backwards. Donald finally called saying the guard wouldn't let him up because it was after hours; I suggested putting the guard on the phone. Explaining what was happening, the guard said he would escort me out of the building. Jackson was not happy with that arrangement.

"Stop right there, Raymond!" Jackson bellowed as the guard approached.

The guard ignored him and stopped at my door. I rose to join him.

"I'm warning you, Raymond, just leave and mind your own business," Jackson threatened, rising to his full height.

Raymond was in his fifties, I'd say, with silver streaks in his black hair, and the top of his head was about even with Jackson's shoulders.

"I believe the young lady wants to leave," Raymond said politely. "And she is signed in; you are not. If there was a fire, no-one would know you are here."

"I'm not done talking to her!" Jackson cried taking a step toward him.

Raymond pulled out his phone to call Donald.

"Mr. Houston," he started, "if your granddaughter is not at your side in 5 minutes, call 911."

Ending the call, Raymond waited for me to come out. I clutched his arm, looking back at Jackson who was livid.

"You're fired, Raymond!" Jackson roared.

"Not such a great job anyway," Raymond muttered to himself.

"Would you want to pack and ship packages?" I quickly asked.

Raymond nodded, looking at me with a smile.

The following Sundays, both Sam and Jackson stayed away which was fine with me. Laura, Abigail and I prayed for both of them to understand their behavior and what God thought of it. Actually, it occurred to me that Jackson might not know God's opinion so I wrote him a short note.

"Dear Jackson,

Because the world today doesn't honor God, I thought I might explain. Hopefully you know there is a commandment that says 'do not commit adultery[11]'. But Jesus said if you <u>look</u> at a woman with lust, you have committed adultery.[12] Furthermore, the Apostle Paul wrote that fornicators[13], or inappropriate sexual behavior, is not allowed into Heaven. 'Inappropriate sexual behavior' is what you have been doing to me.

If you can't understand that, then understand this: I'm following Jesus and he does not want me to fornicate. I will give my body to my husband and no-one else."

A few days later, Jackson called me.

"So what am I supposed to do?" he cried. "These urges are in me!"

Wanting so badly to tell him they were in me too, I stuck to God's script.

"You can ask God to help you," I suggested first. "Read the Bible. Bibles are online or I'll give you one."

My suggestion was met with silence.

"Jackson?" I finally asked.

"I...I have to go," he stated sadly and ended the call.

The next call I got was Davis Jamison who wanted to see me and Andrew agreed to go with me. Greeted by a gentleman at the back entrance of Davis' house, we were taken to a room full of people dressed casually, some in bikinis. The back wall of the room led to a garden with a pool and some were swimming. Jackson, in swim trunks and tee shirt, walked briskly toward us with a beaming smile.

"Hi there," he greeted breathlessly looking at me.

"Hi," I said with trepidation. "Davis asked me to stop by. Was it to see you?"

"Yeah," he said with a laugh and noticing my irritation he added. "It was the only way!"

I looked at Andrew who had disappeared. Sighing, I decided standing in the middle of this room surrounded by these people was my best option.

"Let's go..." Jackson started.

"I'm staying here," I announced flatly.

"Oh, my god, you're ridiculous," Jackson blurted.

"Not in God's eyes. He's saying that about you," I remarked.

Jackson stepped away from me and disappeared into the crowd. I heard Andrew's laugh and he was talking to Sam. About to take a step toward them, Jackson appeared with two kitchen chairs. He sat on one and gently pulled me down on the other. His eyes were pleading with me.

"Baby, you have to come out of the dark ages," he began sincerely. "Living a fantasy is not healthy."

A smile crept onto my face and I couldn't extinguish it. His concern was disarming. Knowing he needed to hear God's word so that faith[14] would grow and that only God could open his eyes[15], I vowed to pray for him diligently until he knew the truth or was no longer breathing.

"Jesus is a historic figure," I answered. "His crucifixion is a fact; his resurrection is a fact; his ascension is a fact. All of these facts can be looked up just like facts about Pele[16]. Did you ever meet Pele? How do you know he existed?"

"You know about Pele?" he gasped.

"Soccer is a big deal in India," I answered. "Much bigger than here."

Davis came out of the crowd with a glass in his hand and chuckled.

"What is this?" he asked and motioned at a butler to take the chairs.

Davis took my hand and walked me toward the pool. I diverted him to Andrew who was laughing with a bikini-clad, well endowed girl.

"Andrew, we need to leave," I stated.

"Oh! Of course," he responded sheepishly, blushing slightly.

Jackson glanced at Davis with a pained look.

"It's too early to leave," Davis whined.

Another well-endowed girl walked to Jackson, saying 'Hi, Honey,' and, facing him, stood as close to him as she could get putting her arms around his neck. When he didn't respond to her, she put his hands on her back and pushed them slowly to her bikini bottoms. Jackson looked at me, face reddened, and withdrew his hands. She looked up at him, then she turned to look at me, the object of his attention. With no words, she walked in front of Jackson toward the pool and made her hand pass very slowly over his groin. He gasped involuntarily. She abruptly grabbed his arm and pulled him into the pool. The onlookers burst into laughter and taunts. In the water, she got on top of him as he struggled to get out. I don't know what happened next because Andrew and I were walking toward the car.

As I drove on the long private lane that led to the street, I saw Jackson running after me at soccer speed. I stopped. Water was streaming off his clothes which was clinging to his muscular chest; cold nipples protruding. I shifted as my groin throbbed.

"You don't have to leave!" Jackson implored.

"I don't belong in a place like that," I explained. "I don't want to belong there."

"Why?" he cried stepping back like I had struck him. "Who's hurting you?"

"That place hurts God," I stated emphatically. "He's not welcome there. I want to be with him."

"Ok. Ok," Jackson said backing away, nodding, like he either understood or gave up. "Live in your fantasy world!" Then he added, "Andrew, Missi wants you to come back. I'll take you home."

"Tell her to come to Sunday dinner," Andrew shouted.

# Chapter 4

With the second year of school underway, my load was heavy with classes and students at the bookstore. Raymond, so excellent with customers, was given Sam's job. Jackson was busy with soccer season so my only glimpse of him was on the big screen. Other suitors came to Sunday dinner but most of them came one time and none of them were interested in attending church.

It was a huge surprise one Sunday when Missi appeared at the door in a white gauze dress with her wavy golden hair touching her tan shoulders. Her smile lit up the room. Andrew was having a hard time squelching his delight and maintaining composure. Andrew was 35 years old and Missi looked young, maybe 20.

After dinner, Andrew and Donald found a game to watch and Abigail, Laura, Missi and I sat outside. Missi eventually spoke of her 'dates' with the soccer players and executives which included sharing her body with them. At Davis' party, in the hour or so that she and Andrew talked, she felt he was not only truly interested in her but also concerned about her. It was a new experience. Laura and I suggested that what she experienced was God's love pouring through Andrew. She responded that she didn't care why, she just wanted to experience it more often. Agreeing to go to church, I arranged to pick her up next Sunday.

On Friday night, Missi called while I was at the bookstore. She had stopped dating and she said her body was craving sex. Offering to take her to dinner, I called Abigail to ask if she would go with us. Abigail, whose husband died in a tragic accident, understood Missi's problem.

"You've got to tell God what you're experiencing, Missi, and be honest," Abigail advised. "God created sex, you know."

"Yes, Adam and Eve," Missi responded. "When my mom first told me about sex, she called Adam a 'baby maker'."

Abigail and I were delighted with that description.

"To this day, I don't watch or read love stories," Abigail explained, "or listen to love songs. I don't want to be aroused."

"Plus, we want to glorify God[17], don't we?" I added. "He isn't glorified with party sex; he is glorified when a man and a woman commit to each other for a lifetime and he blesses that union."

"I wish I had heard those words at your age, Caitlin," Missi sighed. "Jackson doesn't know what he's giving up."

It stung a little to hear 'giving up'. I realized I also had some honest confessions to give to God tonight. On the way home, Abigail said that Andrew was struggling with attraction for Missi.

"Don't mention this to anyone," Abigail disclosed, "but he has been weeping before God. Never have I seen him react to a woman that way."

"Dear God," I said. "Please send me a man like that."

Around 3 AM, Donald answered a knock at the door; it was a patrolman with notification that Sam was in an accident. Before we left for the hospital, Donald wrapped his arms around our shoulders and asked God to heal Sam but also asked for God's will to be done. At the hospital, a doctor came out and said they had done everything possible. We were allowed to look at him through a window as he took his last breath. The pain of separation tore through all of us with deep sobs. Through his tears, Donald listened to instructions from various people then they let us see Sam before he was taken away.

After the funeral, people flocked to our house; Jackson and Missi included. Neighbors had set up a buffet and tables in the back yard. As Andrew and I greeted guests, directing them to the buffet, I saw Missi and Jackson sitting alone, not knowing anyone but us. Telling Andrew where I was going, I sat beside Missi to thank them for coming. Wanting to offer a word of comfort, Jackson stated that Sam was in Heaven. I could have let it go but I wanted him to understand salvation.

"I don't know if Sam ever accepted Jesus as his Savior," I stated with sadness.

"He was a good person," Jackson retorted with a look of shock.

"None of us are good enough," I replied.

"According to who?" Jackson challenged.

"According to God," I answered.

"God is perfection," Missi joined in.

"What!" Jackson cried leaning back. "You, too? I'm outta here!"

Jackson shot out of his chair.

"There goes my ride," Missi stated watching him rush into the house.

"So, you believe in God?" I asked.

"My grandmother was a believer," Missi answered with a sigh. "She took me to church and vacation Bible school whenever she could."

She looked away like she was remembering.

"I don't believe like you do, though," she stated. "You take it seriously."

I nodded, thinking of Jesus on the cross.

"I don't know any girl who can resist Jackson," she continued. "I don't know any girl who can attract him like you do, either."

"Yeah," I sighed. "I don't get it. He's attracted for the wrong reason."

"There have been women like you in history," she mused. "Cleopatra, Helen of Troy..."

"Delilah," I laughed, "all pagan."

"No," Missi retorted. "Who was Abraham's wife?"

"Oh, yeah," I cried. "Sarah[18]. Ninety years old and so beautiful *two* kings took her into the harem! Thanks!"

We laughed and made fun of Abraham for letting the kings take her and Andrew joined us. Missi stretched her hands to him to offer comfort and to my amazement, he took them, starting to weep. Sitting beside him, I gently rubbed his back. Missi was weeping also.

As the house emptied and neighbors helped clean up, I noticed Donald was missing. Walking back toward the family room, I saw Donald and Jackson leaned back in easy chairs. The big screen was on a game but the sound was muted. Andrew and Missi were still outside laughing at something. Looking to Heaven, I prayed for God's will to be done.

The second year of school flew by without incident. Although Jackson didn't come around, Missi was a regular at church and Sunday dinner. As her faith increased along with her knowledge of the Bible, it was clear that she and Andrew were becoming a couple and not surprising when Andrew proposed. Their wedding day was beautiful and fun. As the maid-of-honor, I was busy fulfilling my traditional duties before and during the ceremony and then the traditional photoshoot afterward. At the reception, I was sitting with Missi at the newlywed's table as dinner and cake was served then I was escorted to the dance floor by one of the groomsmen. Without warning, he let go of me and backed away, looking at someone behind me. It was Jackson who took the groomsman's place.

"I...I'm sorry for the intrusion," he began then sighed. "You are so beautiful."

It shocked me that his face puckered - was he fighting tears?

"Are you alright?" I asked.

"I want another chance with you," he stated. "Can I have another chance?"

I didn't know what to say and he took it as rejection.

"How can I earn your trust?" he pressed.

"God will show you how," I advised.

"God?" he started to challenge but immediately backed down.

"Just talk to him," I encouraged softly. "Please."

He stepped back, brought my hand to his lips, kissed it then backed away slowly. Staring at him, I realized I was standing on the dance floor all by myself.

# Chapter 5

A month after their honeymoon, at Sunday dinner, Andrew and Missi announced they were expecting. The joy streaming out of Andrew was palatable and catching. Conversation for the next hour was stories of the family's babies. It made me miss my parents and I thought about visiting them when the school year ended.

Discussing it with Laura and Donald, they thought it was a great idea. My biggest concern was taking care of inventory and taxes at the bookstore. Donald stepped up and said he would handle it. On the day of my flight, they all accompanied me to the airport; I would be gone for three months.

My parents were ecstatic to see me, and I felt the same. They had a party so I could catch up with my friends; some of them being children who had grown into young men and women. We toured the church and school sharing the improvements they had made and what they needed. I realized, with the success of the bookstore, that we should be supporting them.

It was a fast three months and, though hating to leave them, I was glad to be returning to my third year. My flight arrived after midnight and Laura picked me up. She said Donald fell asleep and she didn't disturb him. At home, I also was ready to lie down and I allowed myself to sleep in. Arriving at the store about noon, I brought Donald, Andrew and Raymond some lunch and, as we were eating, I asked if we could support my parents' mission; they agreed wholeheartedly. Donald showed me the status of inventory and the accounts. He had done a good job but he was very happy I was home. As Donald was leaving, Andrew said something about Sunday dinner and Donald replied that Jackson was grilling steaks. I called Laura.

"Grandpa just said that Jackson is grilling steaks!" I exclaimed. "What did he mean?"

"I think he meant that Jackson is grilling steaks," Laura repeated slowly.

"How? I mean, why?" I urged.

"I guess he likes steaks," Laura answered innocently.

"Aaaaghhhh!" I growled.

"What's wrong?" Laura asked.

"Are you kidding me?" I wailed. "Jackson, from out of nowhere, magically starts grilling steaks at Sunday dinner?"

Laura started laughing and laughed for several seconds.

"Jackson has been here every Sunday since you left," Laura explained.

I was mesmerized.

"Caitlin?" Laura said. "Are you still there?"

"Every Sunday?" I stammered. "To see Grandpa?"

"Nooo," she said slowly.

Now she was messin' with me and I decided to stop the game.

"Seriously, Grandma," I begged. "What's going on?"

"Well, your Grandpa told me that Jackson was earning your trust," Laura responded.

All the nerves in my body exploded. My face felt like it was beet red. My groin was pulsing so hard, I was embarrassed.

"Is it for real, Grandma?" I finally ventured to ask.

"I think it is," she answered softly.

Ruined for the day, I told Andrew I was still tired from the trip. Going outside, I started walking, allowing myself, for the first time, to enjoy the memories of Jackson's kiss; his concern when my ankle was broken; his concern that I was living in the dark ages; his parting kiss at the wedding; and, yes, even his groin on my buttocks. Looking to God, I asked him to lead me away from sin, to protect me from sin that wanted to destroy me, to lead me onto the righteous path.

On Sunday morning at church, I gasped when Jackson appeared and sat next to Donald, four people down from me. Peering around Laura, who was sitting next to me, Jackson was talking to Donald, apparently making no effort to get a look at me. Looking to Heaven, I repeated my plea for righteousness to prevail. After service, Jackson drove by himself to the house and he pulled into the driveway after we did. With bags of groceries in his car, we all stopped to help him. He gave me a bag and said my name. I just about fainted.

The men stood around the grill as we ladies cut vegetables. No-one had much to say; there seemed to be a sense of excitement in the air. Missi, at four months, said she was feeling good; that the nursery was ready. Laughter from the men drifted through the sliding glass door.

The steaks were delicious; grilled to perfection. Apparently, this was not the first meal Jackson had prepared for them. He conversed with the ladies about cooking as though he were a chef. After cleaning up, the men found a game on the big screen and Laura, Missi, Abigail and I sat outside. Again, all were quiet.

"Grandma said Jackson has been coming since I left," I started.

"Yeah," Missi marveled. "He showed up one Sunday, unaware you were gone."

"Why didn't he come when I was here?" I asked.

"Soccer," Missi answered flatly.

"Of course," I nodded sheepishly.

The three women knew Jackson wanted to win my hand.

"Is this for real?" I asked them.

"I think it is," Missi answered. "My mom said he has dropped out of the social scene. He practices, goes to team meetings and plays the game. At away games, he eats with the married guys and they watch a movie or play cards, but they don't party like the single guys."

"And I think he's not sure what to do now," Abigail added. "Normally he would take a girl on a date. In Jesus' time, the fathers brought the couple together and the man's father presented the proposal. The girl would accept or reject."

Before leaving, Jackson stopped to say 'good-night'. We all thanked him for a great meal. His eyes rested on me for a moment; I could tell he had to force himself to walk away. That night, Davis Jamison called Donald while we were in the family room. Davis did most of the talking then Donald told me that he and Jackson had a proposal for me. Knowing what that meant, I stopped breathing, eyes widened. Donald asked me if it was ok. I nodded.

The entire week, I struggled to not think about Jackson as I tried to study or work. It helped to read the Bible, pray and listen to my favorite praise and worship songs and ponder what I would wear. I remembered Missi's white gauze dress and she let me borrow it. With a gold cross, I decided it was a perfect look.

At church, like before, Jackson sat next to Donald, four people down from me. This time, I caught him looking at me. Peering around Laura, I smiled and waved my fingers at him. He blushed. His every movement captivated me now. I think I would be happy just watching him do anything.

At the house, Donald and Laura chose to have dinner before presenting the proposal. Davis Jamison carried the conversation with all of his antics. Jackson and I kept glancing at each other, smiling. When the table was cleared, Donald directed Jackson and Davis into the living room. Donald and I stood opposite to them. Everyone else was seated.

Davis pulled a piece of paper from his jacket pocket and started to read. Though I heard a few words, here and there, 'honor', 'devotion', 'provision', all of my attention was on the man who was gazing at me. The love pouring out of him was filling my heart. I knew he would die for me if he had to. When Donald asked me if I accepted the proposal, I said 'I do'. Jackson knelt on one knee, opened a black box, took my hand and slid his engagement ring on my finger. He then handed a ring to me. I knelt, took his hand, and slipped an engagement ring onto his finger. Standing up, everyone applauded then the men watched a game and we ladies made wedding plans.

He called me that night to thank me for accepting his proposal. I thanked him for making it. I shared ideas for the wedding and he hoped that I would take care of all that, except he would arrange the honeymoon. He also told me he had to leave for Europe on a business trip and would be back in a few weeks. He called me every night after that; sometimes during the day. I was fully occupied with making the wedding arrangements and, by the way, Missi had her baby.

At our wedding, the traditional rituals ruled the agenda and the entire ceremony was beautiful. When the pastor said, 'you may now kiss the bride', Jackson and I stepped toward each other as we rehearsed. He put his arms around me and got his face as close to me as he could without touching me.

"Aren't you going to kiss me?" I whispered.

"If I kiss you, I won't be able to stop," he whispered back.

"Ok, let's face the congregation so he can pronounce us man and wife," I urged. "Then we can go to the reception."

"I don't want to go to the reception," he stated firmly.

"We have to go to the reception!" I blurted, trying to keep my voice down.

The pastor stepped toward us.

"Is there a problem?" he asked.

Jackson looked at him, heaved me over his shoulder and rushed down the aisle.

"Caitlin!" Laura cried amid laughter, gasps and whistles from the congregation.

"I guess we're leaving!" I shouted, laughing.

I hurled my bouquet into the congregation. Then I pulled off my veil and flung it toward a little girl. She squealed with delight.

"What time is the flight?" I asked Jackson, assuming he arranged the honeymoon.

"We're going home," he answered, as though I had just asked him the time.

He put me in the car and closed the door. My family and friends were on the lawn waving, laughing and wishing us well. As we drove toward 'home', wherever that was, I could not think of a reason for stopping him. He wanted intimacy and he had waited years for this moment.

He pulled into an estate that took my breath away. Thinking it was a resort, I was corrected quickly when he unlocked the door and carried me across the threshold. The stunning hardwood floors led straight to an outer area with a breathtaking mountain view. On the left was a bar. On the right, a cozy seating area, where he put me down.

He took off his jacket and pulled his tuxedo shirt over his head, leaving his tie on his neck. Unbuckling his pants, they fell to the ground. I watched him with wonder, not interfering, until he struggled getting his briefs down. I kneeled and gently, slowly pulled them down to his feet. He was captivated, gazing at me with wonder. And, there it was, the baby maker, poised for action. Having seen drawings in biology books and only a few actual pictures, I touched him. He shuddered and laid me back.

Turning me over he fumbled with the first of twenty fabric-coated buttons then he ripped the rest, making buttons fly everywhere. I was hysterical with laughter. Turning me over again, he wasn't laughing. The intensity of his concentration was striking. Taking ahold of my top, he pulled it back like he was opening a treasure chest. His eyes widened at what he saw. With the tips of his trembling fingers, he felt my skin and what he was doing became serious to me.

Continuing down my body with his fingers, he gently pushed my dress down, taking time to feel every square inch. Still with a gentle, slow motion, he pushed my panties down and stopped with my dress around my knees. He studied my crotch in the same way I studied him and touched me. I gasped. He bent down to caress my lips for several seconds.

Removing my dress, he felt the skin on my legs and made his way up my thigh back to my groin. Finally, he put his thighs under mine, touched my groin with his baby maker and my head exploded. Never had my body felt a sensation like this. Gasping with every move, I realized this was God's design; this was God's way of making babies and I marveled that he made it so beautiful.

We filled our home with God's Word, God's love and five babies. When Jackson retired from soccer, his wealth allowed him to be home with the children and me. As our children grew into their teens, he insisted that all 'dating' occur with a parent present. We visited my parents in India several times and he used his fame to speak at churches about the mission and how God changed him from a playboy to a born-again believer. He preached to fathers to protect their daughters and to instill in their sons the importance of abstinence. He admitted with embarrassment that he had physical relations with a number of women but, it was his relationship with me, a Godly woman, that was fulfilling, satisfying and enduring.

Proverbs 31:10-12 KJV "Who can find a virtuous and capable wife? She is more precious than rubies. Her husband can trust her, and she will greatly enrich his life. She brings him good, not harm, all the days of her life."

[1] John 3:8 KJV "The wind bloweth where it listeth, and thou hearest the sound thereof, but canst not tell whence it cometh, and whither it goeth:"

[2] Matthew 5:28 KJV "But I (Jesus) say unto you, That whosoever looketh on a woman to lust after her hath committed adultery with her already in his heart."

[3] KJV

[4] John 3:5-7 KJV "5 Jesus answered, Verily, verily, I say unto thee, Except a man be born of water and of the Spirit, he cannot enter into the kingdom of God. 6 That which is born of the flesh is flesh; and that which is born of the Spirit is spirit. 7 Marvel not that I said unto thee, Ye must be born again."

[5] GED - General Education Development. A high school diploma granted when required tests are passed.

[6] Romans 5:12 KJV "Wherefore, as by one man sin entered into the world, and death by sin; and so death passed upon all men, for that all have sinned:"

[7] Psalm 51:5 KJV "Behold, I was shapen in iniquity; and in sin did my mother conceive me."

[8] Romans 1:18 KJV "For the wrath of God is revealed from heaven against all ungodliness and unrighteousness of men, who hold the truth in unrighteousness;"

[9] Romans 5:9 KJV "Much more then, being now justified by his blood, we shall be saved from wrath through him."

[10] John chapter 3

[11] Exodus 20:14 KJV "Thou shalt not commit adultery."

[12] Matthew 5:28 KJV "But I (Jesus) say unto you, That whosoever looketh on a woman to lust after her hath committed adultery with her already in his heart."

[13] I Corinthians 6:9-10 KJV "Know ye not that the unrighteous shall not inherit the kingdom of God? Be not deceived: neither fornicators, nor idolaters, nor adulterers, ...shall inherit the kingdom of God."

[14] Romans 10:17 KJV "So then faith cometh by hearing, and hearing by the word of God."

[15] Acts 16:28 KJV Jesus speaking to Paul: "To open their eyes (the Gentiles), and to turn them from darkness to light, and from the power of Satan unto God, that they may receive forgiveness of sins, and inheritance among them which are sanctified by faith that is in me (Jesus)."

[16] Pelé was a Brazilian professional footballer who played as a forward.

[17] 1 Corinthians 10:31 KJV "...whatsoever ye do, do all to the glory of God."

[18] Genesis 12:10-20 and 20:1-18

www.ingramcontent.com/pod-product-compliance
Lightning Source LLC
Chambersburg PA
CBHW051301160726
47994CB00003B/1271